all the places
we don't
want to go

All The Places We Don't Want To Go

Gabriel Ògúngbadé

FABULA/Plays
an imprint of
Abibiman Publishing

New York & London

First published in Great Britain in 2022 by Abibiman Publishing
www.abibimanpublishing.com

All rights reserved. Published in the United Kingdom by Abibiman
Publishing, an imprint of Abibiman Music & Publishing, London.

Abibiman Publishing is registered under Hudics LLC in the United
States and in the United Kingdom.

ISBN: 978-1-9989958-4-4

Cover design by Gabriel Ogungbade.

"Life can only be understood backwards; but it must be lived forward."

– Søren Kierkegaard

for my mother

Contents

Bleak Sundara

To paint on a nonexistent canvas.
To dance to an internal, one-sided song.
To shatter the empty glass.
To burn the wax wings in breathless descent.

Do we laugh, smile, or cry?
as we fumble through tangles.
Do we pray, curse, or chide?
as we cradle the scorpion under a broken wing.

The husk,
the self-paradise;
the own purgatorio,
the bleak Sundara.

reflected in our scars

when do we start living? he asked,
dried up before flickering screens
soaked in expensive sewage
broken down in a loveless life...
there's life but there's no living,
he said.

it's funny
how,
a tiny bed
and a flat pillow
is enough to
contain
a sack of dry
memories,
a life of dank
compromise
and a full head
of frail hair...

the same words, different days,
always the same people, he said.

I know, I reply
So, I turn away from the mirror
and return to this tiny bed,
to this cracked smartphone
and this stale life...

2

the words in my heart
grow thin and die
before they even touch
my notebook...

my eyes are heavy,
my face is stiff,
I'm broke
but my pockets
are full.

jigsaw

wandering away
from adventure.
washing down
lies with burning
whisky.
finding balance
in one-sided
affection.
finding balance
in the things
that makes you
sick
to your gut.
one foot in
the past,
the other in tomorrow;
not knowing where
you stand.
  hurting the ones
who love you.
  those wise eyes of
a coward under
sunken cheeks.

you hide behind
weak rigour,
could swear you
love the things
you despise

and you accept
the love you think
you deserve...

why would he
make us so
incomplete?

show me to the fire

you tumbled down
the mountain.
your blood blessed
this communion.
your bone is
my bone.
my eyes are
your eyes.
I am one of your
voices.

you devour yourself
only to birth
yourself again.
this daily
loop.

bringer of light,
who am I?

finding star

you showed me
to parts of
myself I
didn't know were
missing.
filled the abandoned
terrain with your
tangerine beauty.
[red lips,
face of a greek
goddess, soft honey
voice].

the lost piece
of a
one-sided coin;
bone of my
bone.

your name was on
my tongue
when I travelled
that lonely road
to this bleak
paradise.

you, my star,
are the home
I came here
to
discover...

7

feather in the machine

it was like a
cheap trick;
one second
I was a boy,
the next I'm
stumbling drunk
into bed, hoping
the day was
a nightmare...

it knows
just how to
beat us down.

it's a dry day
in my mid-twenties;
numb teeth and
aching ankles,
I'm staring down
at a worn heap of
folds and lumps
(bony legs and a
hairy chest)
and out the corner
of my eyes,
I see it;
mechanical face,
voice like the tick
of a clock,
telling me

to go on
to push further;
one more second,
one more hour,
one more month,
one more boring
commute to classrooms,
to laboratories,
to half-hearted words
and radiated dreams
one more tiring
day of work,
one more pose
for people I don't
know,
one more wasted
youth...

it knows
just how to
beat us down.

people like us

…it's the unspoken
bond we share,
say, standing
in line by an
atm machine.
or those wise
conversations
with a fellow
bus commuter…
    that general
diplomacy inside
a local bank.
[like sitting at a
dinner table with
these strangers,
your temporary
siblings].

hot afternoon,
waiting under
the shade.
worried I've
over-spent.
worried I'm
late.

worried about
my tiny bladder.
darned worry
is a bitch.
but it's
something
we
share.

happy is a dying breed

some drunk sleeping
on street corners.
these bone thin boys
making sand castles.
all those
one-squared meals.
    Coldplay sang
of
paradise.

over here,
we build our
castles on
the
inside
and leave
all the ugly
outside.

all the jailhouses,
madhouses and
burial grounds
are full,
happy is a
dying breed.
and I used to
be full of
life.
before life
happened.

but you enjoyed the rust

you strike a match,
touch the flame
to a firecracker,
point it up
to a moody sky;
BANG!
your joints
trembled with
joy.
the smell of ozone
tingled your sinuses.

harmattan days were
dry, quiet, cosy;
sweaters and balmed lips...
door locks stiffened,
wet clothes dried too fast,
and sweat tingled your skin
like little cupid kisses...

but you enjoyed the rust,
the dust,
the boredom,
the dusty streets
and your cracked lips,
you traced stars with
freezing fingers
on stuffy nights

and slept under
lukewarm wrappers.

you find Decembers
dull nowadays;
there are no more
harmattan days...

the weight of our memories

I'm scared I'll break
under the weight of
the memories
we created...
or maybe I'll tear
my mind apart
for the ones
we left unborn;
her perfect bum-crack
under ripped jeans,
her burning temper,
those peach-juicy
breasts...

ice cream dripping
down her chin
like a star's teardrop,
I swear I could just
lean in and —
shit!

I vomit all the memories;
good, bad, burning temper,
perfect bum-crack and
dripping ice cream:
I pile them up
in my sink and
light a bonfire...

11pm, I'm soapy under
a broken shower,
I'll probably walk out
dirtier than I entered;
it's this muddy water,
it's this tired world...
    the memories will
crawl back into
my dreams
and I'll probably get
drunk again tomorrow.

an unwritten idea

the sun wakes to my empty bed,
last night's tears still wet the pillowcase
and the reek of vomit sits lonely in the air...
stillborn words hang loose on an open page
as spider-webs reclaim the empty spaces
between my books...
my mirror watches the lonely tree
sitting outside the window,
hanging his head in silent reflection — his leaves
are shrivelled pale papers (but new leaves would not
bloom) ...
the old clock continues his morose march to infinity,
dragging his old feet through circular days;
wrra wrra wrra
and on my desk sits your torn heart;
tainting the pages blood-crimson and pumping
the air with the dank sickness of putrefaction.
on my desk sits your torn heart,
an unwritten idea...

a gift

the cosy night
after a rainstorm —
watching a
pear tree mature in
your front yard —
fingers splintered
by chipped wood —
firecrackers in
December —
bird nest by
the window —
a small green-yellow
snake on a branch —
   our childhood years
are alternate worlds
of magic,
youth is anxiety
and clenched teeth
and adulting is
Dante's nightmare...
we are seeds
that only grow
into trees
from six feet
under.

where were you
before you even
existed?
what were those

first seconds like?
who held your
hands when you
took those first
steps?

you don't get to
choose your father,
and your mum
is a precious gift
from the cosmic.

we're all going there (i)

lumbering forward in a
meatsack as I
grunt greetings
to strangers.
[dying in trickles]
    my father walked
this path
and so will my daughter…
we're running away
from something,
towards something,
eventually towards that
rectangular hole in
the family plot.

I belong nowhere.
I am as I appear.
    I am, and
    I am not.

that was the wildest feeling

there's a
certain
joy
that comes
with unloading
the weight
of
a full day
of drinking
into a porcelain
goalpost.

when standing
upright
is a stellar
achievement
and
you're humming
an old tune
under your
breath,
ignoring the
suspicious
frowns
as you wash
your hands
at the bathroom
sink.

they don't
know how
happy it
feels to
not remember
your problems.
   ahh, who cares
about *they*
anyways?

becoming a hero

i
the world
continues
beyond
a covered
window…
fear on
the evening
wind;
whispers of
a war,
more boys
to be
sacrificed
at some
coward's
whim.
   and I'm just
a sag on
my chair.
the god
of roaches
and rats.

it's hard to
break that
stance,
when your
eyes are slits
under the

23

bedsheet.
   finger
tracing circles
on a beer can.
this writhing
blanket of
ants on a
used plate.
blades slicing
stale air
overhead.

ii
some days,
each thought
is another
musing
into the
cemetery within
and the most
heroic thing
you can do
is crawl out
of bed to
piss.

a game you play

push, elbow, run,
we don't walk here...
dude, we should only smile,
cry,
anger
behind screens
    but we carry the stiffness
into our hearts...
(factory joy)

love is your puppet,
a game you play.

they don't see you;
you're just a face,
just another mask.

you're home,
you're lost.
"what's on your mind?"

THIS lonely JOURNEY

pluck these thorns
from my
scalp.
bury my pain
and suck
the poison
from my veins –

show me
the source
of my misery
and leave me
here,
in my youth,
with my beer
and my books,
and my guilt.

tell the world
that I tried.
but these battles
are mine
to fight
alone.

I seek to
conquer
myself.

good things end too early

…she didn't explain,
didn't need to;
Mr. Law had
hunt down
and skinned
her business.
bloody typical.

the rice is bland
now,
turkey over-fried,
beans undercooked
and there's simply
no fried plantain,
the symphony
has left
her food.
    she didn't
explain though,
didn't need to;
places like these
don't belong
beside a
restless
road.

advise to a Wallflower

if you become
wary of life;
do the moonwalk
on an expressway.
swagger naked
into a full
classroom.
    drink gasoline.
wear your shirt
backwards
and start
your sentences
midway…
    to those
self-help books
that tell you to
'embrace the
chaos,'
I say
try narrating
your heartache
to a
deaf
musician…

nameless onez

you'll find them
backstage,
tinkering.
   in the liquor aisle,
taking hasty notes.
   under the shade,
   watching the
picture
get taken.
you'll find them
eating
with the 'good ones'
inside swaying,
famished trees.

   …where the crowd is
at its lowest.
   the music at its finest.
   …those cracks where gods
sneak through.

don't cry, mama

it stood in
my glow,
face of a
cherub,
and drank
from my
cup.
drank
my blood.
it ate from
me and
ate at me.

it wore
my skin.

it kills me,
this dream,
this horror
of mine.
it kills me.
   and
it is the
reason
I still live.

We'll Never Know

"What was your first impression of me?"
"Curious."
"Curious? How?!"
"Well, I've learned not to trust beautiful things."

that was
the beginning,
middle,
end
of a love story
that never happened.

...but agony needs our permission

his teeth were
black
and dead,
eyes scampering
in their sockets
like rats and
he smelled like
a corpse,
"Fine boy, give
us money," he said.

but I was in debt
and
I either pay for
affection or sit
beside HER grave
and rant.

slapped his palm
with a N100,
winked and
swaggered away
laughing and
laughing
and
laughing.

wake up, it's time to dream

break off your
antlers and
paddle into
that dead
night…
 hunt your
devils and
slit their
throats.
bathe in your
own white
fire.

crumple the beer cans…
crush the A4s…
burn the wax…
drench the pillowcase
with tears and
anxiety…
bury your dreams
in sleepless nights…

find what you love
and let it
kill you…

the gods are
waiting
for you…

mellow orbiting

those blank, unworried
eyes,
morning sun peeks
from above,
a timid fairy flowing
through a patch
of white pollen.
[slippery rubber
slippers, bunny-tied
hair;
a blissful, strange
figure beside a
gushing tap].
   and the neighbour's
dog barks, hungry.
and I'm an ornament
rocking on a brick
wall.

--

I could show you
my cave,
my scribbled
delusions,
dog-eared books.
   two nesting birds
under warm
duvet.

[two angels
kneeling before
a tree-tall pendant.]

--could trundle this
abandoned path
with you under
my wing.

if the words
haven't left.

--
and in our
flounder,
sparks darting
around,
fleeting glances
and noncommital
nods,
in our callous
dance,
the sunflowers dance.
and the pidgeons
bicker.
and I long for
the spaces
you left your
soft prints.

--

if you come
again,
bring your
soft smile,
your radiance.

nothing shines
so innocent
anymore.

Apollo is silent

agony,
always agony…
   I must be
missing
something.
must be
doing
something
wrong,
   a fatal
        flaw?

or maybe I
just
don't belong
here,
was brought
here against
my will.
   can only
count the
seconds,
(slowly peel
my skin)
as I crawl
closer
to
home.

what do I call you?

I'd like to wake up
with the taste of
last night's kiss
on my lips,
away from friends
that are not friends,
smiles that are not
smiles
away from a body
I don't recognise
and a life
I've been tasked to live...

I'd like to wake up
early in life
and see you again with
eyes that are warm
and a heart that's not
asleep...

Your glistening skin
under the murky wash
of streetlights,
the clasp of your body
on mine,
your lisp:
I still see you
when my eyes
are closed
(stuck in amber).

It's 3 am; old lightbulbs
outside my window.
A dying city
at my doormat.
I'm sleeping awake
in a nondescript
body,
watching for your
reflection
in these words
I've written.

why wake up

you're an explosion
of activity on some
Wednesdays,
a sober wreck
on some Mondays,
a nervous roadkill
on certain days.
and Sundays
are for rice,
boredom and
hatched pods
of baby anxiety
seeds...

you're searching for
bliss in coffee mugs and
rehearsed affection.

somehow, you've
chosen to walk in
tight loops and
your wardrobe is
lined with
personalities...

your dreams
are free only
when you're
asleep...

why wake up?

boy, it's easy to be you

you comb
your mane,
brush your
beard,
rub your
beard,
rub on the
deodorant
and scowl
into the mirror,
aftershave sharp
on stale air.
--a man,
that's what
you are.

those unpaid
debts make
your stomach
churn.
where's the
money coming
from?
--baby on the
way.
    well it's not
easy being a
man.

roaring down
the street,
iron gators,
eyes hidden
under ray bans,
swagger and
smooth.
--a man.
   swallow your
opinions.
choke on my
pride.
sleek and crass.
could grill your
turkey on
my temper.
MAN.

you arrive at
work,
shed the
fabric
and sink
into uniform.
big crude
security guard;
watchful
protector of
gamblers,
addicts,
harlots,

degenerates
and screw-ups.

man
man
man.

the delusions we sacrifice

they remind me of
the freshness
of morning,
the decay
of wilted
petals.

their ache
resounding in
my chest, through
my shell and into soft
flesh... a biting rhythm,
a hollow pang.

--

those snuffed lights
reaching stubbornly
through time... into
the suffocating night.
an expanding cosmos
of dying and rebirthing
beauty...

--

tiny fingers
under
packed earth...
    they weep their

44

songs to deaf
ears...
dreams left
unexplored.

they   whisper
their reproach
to me in my
sleep.

--all those stolen
little lights.

we're all going there (ii)

my demons
are stronger…

these battles
are not mine
to conquer
and
this fight
(called life)
will see
no winner
no loser…

the earth will
consume all
that walks
this path…

memento
memento.

solitary one (a loner in uni)

you still walk
with your emotional
hands stuck in
your pocket.
you don't know
where to correctly
place your words
and you've never
chewed raw noodles
for lunch.

you're not
one of us
if you fly cabs,
if you don't see
long walks as
sacred practice.

if your *Nike Slides* aren't
bleeding fresh,
your tote bag isn't
dope
and you haven't
a 'boo'.

you're not
one of us

because you don't
speak
our language...

you're a
solitary one.

sweaty titan

I don't recall birth,
I don't think of it,
I don't think;
I eat, rest, flutter
on awkward
wings and
lurk behind a
massive machine.

there was another one,
a tall one;
he was slow, graceful,
terrifying, loud
and sublime.
a god...

we lived divided
in our little universe;
he left me offerings
and I sang him
praises
in his sleep...

found me
devouring an offering,
he howled in delight,
slapped at me
(hard).

something broke, something hurt
I flew,
and
he chased;
graceful, slow,
terrifying and godlike.

he slapped again,
I cracked open,
I flew,
he didn't chase,
didn't need to;
I flew out of my body...

I was goop
on the carpet
and he was a
sweaty titan...
I felt like colour.

he saw me, he saw through me
he walked through me,
he didn't look back...

the little things we cherish

His wife is trapped
in a box under
rented earth, her skin
returned to dust.
He collects valuables,
travels with a dirty
teddy bear on his
work rounds and
his little Bimpe
is a simple blot
of joy on a
barren canvas.

He smokes cigarettes under
hot sun,
barely flinches when
spirit burns his tongue
(or his wounds) …
His palms are calloused
leather,
voice the scrape of gravel,
and the black webs on his
feet carry venom to his heart,
but his little Bimpe is
at the top of her class
and nothing (not even arthritis)
can kill that happiness.

His truck is overflowing
with nylon wrappers, discarded electronics
plastic containers, rubber whatevers
and receipts:
everything we once
cherished…

He collects valuables…

huBari's Labyrinth

my bones are rumbling,
medusa snakes dancing
to the wind's cry and
the motorbike's engine
is a cricket's
monologue.

fast and fast
and fast and
fast; we've
found balance
in danger…

the muezzin call…
concrete grassland…
a wise old beggar…
old naira bills…
a wandering magician,
steady red eyes
and aching joints.
who are these people
and what are we
running from?

I get so small

when I close
my eyes
I get small,
I get so small
I could be
another grain
of sand
in your shoe,
so small
you could wipe
me off your
cheek,
so small
you could forget
me in last week's
jeans
so small
I could dissolve
on your
tongue...

small enough
to fit
in the crack
on your heart...

we walk fast,
talk fast,
love fast,
love too fast,

then hate later;
when our heart
rips apart.
we live fast
but we're not
moving.
we're saying so much
but we're not
talking.
you, me, her;
we're drunk on
bottle-nose
perspectives.

what a life.

love is that
painful pang of
sweetness
I can't touch.
and life is darker
when my eyes
are open.

blooming planet

I know you
like I know
my name.
like a
foetus
knows
its womb.
like a peacock
knows its
radiance.

--

I plucked the
secrets you
hide under
your tongue
with my
tongue.

those days I
toiled with the
tigers in my
head as you
emerge from
warm milk.

--

...this
blossoming
star, your arms
around me;
our dolphin
dance.

--

the body of
our tangible
romance.
the fire
burning
behind our
rib cages.
the cord
that binds
us into
infinity.

my tangerine
queen.

we're operating on information

sledgehammer knocks
on my door,
my name rolls out
with the hangman's
rotten breath.
my heart already
jumped out the
window…
"Please come with us."

a silent stride towards
certain trouble; stone-faced…
a full bladder…
tapping out a tune from
anxiety's hymn book.
6 am, I'm clawing
back at the screech
behind my eyes…
my gaze lands on everything
but the dangling handcuffs.

that mocking music
lurking beyond sight.
those beady eyes of
a rat in a trap.

"Piss inside this cup."

a sick, old man,
a vomiting schoolgirl,
a fevered sportsman
and empty-faced nurses;
there is no pity
for the weak.

"I'll have fun writhing about this,"
I told myself...
It's not fun.
It's not happy-sad.
There is no fun
in shame and
suffering.

The machine feeds
on my time,
but I win
every time I pick
up my pen...

interstellar ritual

the moon is void tonight (detached)
so, in my sleep,
I'll swim the rings of Saturn…

falling
rising

mother is born again tonight,
dancing and twisting
and twisting and dancing
in her shawl of darkness.

watching ghosts crawl

Watching her tumble
in the sun;
I wonder if she still
recalls the boredom
of early life:
sleepy evenings and
dragonflies after
rainfall…

these men, they crawl
over her skin,
they poke her,
they eat her children
and leave her
plastic offerings.

nothing to show
of this sunbeaten
beauty but a flat
breast and seaweeds
where her fingers
touch the sky.
nothing to see
but tiring vigour.

mosquito bites…
a prancing crab…
new leaves on a
frail trunk…
some lonely flowers…

Squirrels dancing
to my music,
to love's music.
   yes, this is where
artists call home:
a garbage can
for emotions…

bits

barefoot on warm tar,
moonlight on water ripples.
tears or shower-water?
blisters are salted and
the same song is
left on repeat...
my ache is something
gifted-wrapped...

   a fresh pose…
toothpick eyelashes...
combed sideburns and
an elastic smile;
you spend your
waking moments
on a tightrope...

these streets suffocate
us;
fallen starfishes
crawling along
the seabed.
   drowning in
this collective
illusion.

home

we are not much,
she and I,
we are not
mighty,
not small;
we are what
we are…
   this little place
is nondescript,
but it's ours
and everything
else
is noise.

an aftertaste

face on the sunny
ocean line,
buttons undone
on my threadbare shirt,
sand tickling the spaces
between my toes as
I pick seashells
with her;
    a few cans of
beer can really
get you dreaming...

the price of daydream
is the freefall return
to reality   and hope
is a two-faced
coward...

it's true that love
is all we need,
but my heart is
a can of worms and
my attention is salt.
    10:11pm, alone in
my crowded dorm-room,
I've pushed her away,
but the daydreams
are my obsession...

know

how to
separate
alone from
lonely.

don't go
to
extremes.

bread, for the evening

evening wind,
wet clothes flapping
on the line.
weak light on
the street.
shadows gesturing
on windows,
orange generator
lights.

…crossed the street.
bought
coconut bread.
this windswept
road makes
you feel alone
inside your
own body;
    a tree on
some maize farm.

you spat,
dug your feet
and walked into
that
cold freezer,
    some call it
life.

same time tomorrow?

we all have
that look,
the one you
make in an
empty room,
when the
outside
threatens to
break into you.
   it's a sacred
arrangement
of facial
muscles.
a gesture
we can't
identify.

   bending
into shapes
and sizes
until the core
forgets its
mother's
face;
it's a curse
whispered
when
no one
is
looking.

loca-loco

I'm a barfly
In this
red red
bar
called mosaic.
there's a bulging
bag of
plantain chips
on my table.
[yellow stripes
on the walls].
   my tumbler is
full of
beer,
and reality
is cramming
itself
into
every
conflicted
thought I
carry.

I often
get tired
of me.

emotional haircut

happiness is a lonely Monday,
a good book of spellbinding fiction,
a belly-full of crappy coffee
and *indomie noodles*.

my personal boredom
lifts my heart
upon a setting sun
(a happy-sad soundtrack
between quiet walks)
   but it is mine,
I created this happiness
and it is mine
alone.

all the firsts

if history truly
repeats itself,
then I can't wait
to meet you again
for the first time.
hold you for the
first time.
fight with you
for the first time.
I'd like to feel
all the firsts
again
and then
get bored of you
get bored with you,
escape the world
with you in my
passenger seat.

old friends we
don't talk to.
family we avoid.
rich friends we
pretend to love.
and kids we'd
kill for...

you broke through
my walls like
the first rays
of dawn.

I tore you open,
fingered your pages,
saw your dreams
your fears
your flaws.

I kissed your tears.
God wrote a masterpiece.

golden leaves

early mornings...
meeting rooms...
raw lungs and
busy streets...

burnt out in
front of laptop
screens...

everyone fills
you up with
noise.
everyone wants
something from
you and, eventually
everyone leaves
[this decrepit
crossroads]...

family says I need
more friends but
what do they
know about
this lonely
madness?
this great
white noise
within?

the air is
clean,
for now,
and I'm just
another golden
leaf littering
the lawn.

our blood. our bone. our flesh. our...

Our path takes us down the gullet of monsters
and up the courtyard of kings. We walk amongst
vile ugliness cloaked in beauty. We walk amongst
light resigned to shadows… We walk –
and walk –
and keep walking.
For the road is hungry for the inner-self. Hungry
for the light behind our eyes. The road feeds on
our smiles.
So, we walk and run, and run and walk –
Smiling less and walking more –
We stumble on doubts, eat our fears and trip on
love. We live in phases, much like the moon. Our
dreams are smeared across the stars.
When the road gets dark; grows thorns. Light
shines in through our cracks; cloaks us. But
through it all, we walk –
and walk –
and keep walking.
(It is such that we suck on blood, caked under our
fingernails)
I do not know which of us wrote this.

restless, under the hibiscus

saw a dead bird
in my backyard,
legs pointing
upwards
in praise.
[old chirper is free]
   I buried it.
sat myself beside
this heap of sand
and drank
shamelessly-cheap
wine.

that dry patch,
under the hibiscus
shade
summons me
every evening.
so, I move
my drinking
and my writing
there.

can't tell if
that bird's
restless soul
craves company
or if I'm
just
fxxking
lonely.

boiling over

I've been there,
and, I think,
we've all
been there;
eyes wide,
wild,
raving mad
in an aimless
fight
when the
real battle
is an ache
inside..
early January,
the kind of
afternoon that
ends under a
cold shower
with you
scrubbing off
the day's stain…
some frustrated
university staff
screaming at me
in a school cab.
"Don't touch me
with your bag!"
"I wasn't planning on that"
"This is arrogance!"
"What?!"

poor man was
underpaid,
ignoring this simple
truth;
the university screws
us all;
lowly staff, student, lecturer,
lab instructors and
those valiant cleaners;
we are all screwthings.

"Alright, I'm sorry… I'm sorry!"
his anger cracked,
face twitching…
he lapsed into
a confused silence.
I scraped away from
him.
He continued
grumbling,
stubborn old tiger…

Times like these
we need to be
left alone with
our personal
devils.

some-how?

some watch sports.
some run their nose
along lines of snow
"This is the last time."
some trade relationships
like underwear.
some work like machines
and there are those who
prefer the underbelly of
bridges to constipated offices.
   I crack a beer and
increase the volume
of music when life
gets too loud…
some hide their sanity
inside a box and
smash
smash
smash the key to it.
   some hide themselves
in words, pages, bottles,
loose clothing
and staff rooms…
some burn their brand
on the face of weaklings,
eat their food
and sleep in
their nest.

some pour all their *Me*
into a tribe of wolves.
some let life beat them
into a shallow grave...

how do you cope?

slept on concrete

woke up to Harper Lee's words,
something must have
died and decomposed
in my mouth
but I only slept two hours.
the banshee in my head
would not stop screeching and
an old drunk laughs at me
through the mirror.
*(of a morning born in
Kafka's hallucinations).*
    But Lee's works are original.
she's warm and tough, her
words pulling you in;
a mother's embrace.

past the gate,
into the snake's jaw,
I pay children
for safe passage.
walked through smoke,
    through mirror.
touched the 'Do Not Touch(s)'
sipped my favourite poison
and watched night
swallow the sun
beside a gurgling
pond.
I read poetry to a graveyard
and played dead amongst

the living.
yes, it's easy to live
when everyone
around you
are busy
dying.

at home, with the red crabs

we sat there
for a while,
alone and incomplete,
but together,
beside a
restless
lagoon.

that space
where mother left
empty,
where the other
lovers planted
a cemetery;
we sat there
and watch
the waves
roll…

you brought daylight
to this place,
brought something
it needed.
so, now, the old
clock wouldn't
move his hands
and the waves
are slowly
erasing
me —

crusader nectar

do you remember
the time I told you
that you were the best
I ever had?
I meant it.

same as I meant it
when I told her
and *her*
and *her*
and *her*…

there is no escape
from hotel receptions;
dancing around the
flower to the melody
of tasteless
small talk;
"Same room as last time?"

there is no escape
from waterfronts;
pleading with
the sidewalkers
(the goddess' minions)
to carry my prayers
of purity
of repentance

and abnegation
to the ear
of the river…

I'm staring blank-faced
Into a pristine pane
of madness.
this feeling will pass
and I will sink
my teeth
into *her*
again…

barracuda (edges of life)

the waves are
stampeding
water horses.
bipolar wind
pats my cheek
as the stamping hooves
vanish into
frothy steam.

there's a blinking
light in the distance;
muffled like a boxed
voice in a coffin.
I'm crawling sideways
towards salty peace.
I'm riding on clouds
of beer
and my tongue
sits on the line
where water meets
sky.

In my drunken
delight, I wonder
if this is where
God lives.
I wonder if he
looks at me
across the
silky waves

and tips his
plastic cup
in salute...
if he lives on
the razor
edges of life,
where peace
and madness
sit to eat.

a taste of honey

i
rainstorm for
seven days.
blistering sun
baked the street
clay afterwards…
    balmy harmattan
nights.
…buzzing beetles in
makeshift sandal
cages.
--small world,
cowpea world.

ii
that insufferable
alarm screeches.
you fumble into
uncertain days.

hereditary misery;
our disorder is
inbred, native
and escape trails
a rebellious path;
swaggering against
the grain.

lonely walks,
crowded streets…

feverish, crummy days,
untidy ego,
why did I stop
to drink the
false ichor?

iii
a small room.
her face glowed
(a candy-sweet sunflower),
gold-brace lines
the bottom row
of her teeth…

"you are safe
here."
the air closed
over her words.
purple braids cascading
over honey-yellow
shoulders.
    a tingling (electric)
current in the air.

time spread its
wings, trickled
fast and fast
into evening.
[folding into
day's close].

peace poured from
her, long and deep.
am I dreaming awake?

iv
there is a
unhinged stranger
in the mirror —
long hours spent
planting flowers
in the cemetery
inside me —

weak wings
manoeuvring
a monsoon;
an unfeeling,
unfriendly,
unconscious
society.

--

her saccharine,
soft embrace,
her delicate arms
wrapped around
me;

that's home.
for
now.

these words are stillborn

I rub these words together,
searching for a faint spark —

I crawl through old papers,
looking for that early magic —
I scoop themes in my palms
and watch them crumble apart... |

my pen stutters over an open page
as my mind screams silent havoc —

these very words are dying
before they are born...

Acknowledgments

my life is pocked with ups and downs; a vibrant, unpredictable landscape of chaos, beauty, magic and books. i cannot help but look back and remember with wild affection all those who, somewhere along the way, have helped lighten the load (of such a caustic life).

much gratitude must go to the following incredible goons:

Onyeka Nwelue, for taking a chance on me (and my book). believing in me when everyone else abandoned -- for being a formidable beacon of light when the storm-darkness ravages. for refining me into a better artist...

my entire family (especially my three sisters, who raised me to be the affectionate man I am today).

Daniel Kazmaier (founder and Editor-in-chief of Our Verze Magazine), the first person to ever publish me. for believing in my art... some poems in this volume first appeared in Our Verse Magazine.

the Adeduros, for tolerating my wild, rogue nature, taking care of me when darkness almost engulfed me. for the endless love and support.

Koye Atoyebi, some friends are closer than family; maybe water is thicker than blood?

Toyin Akinosho, for your fatherly love. for paving the

way for young creatives. for being a role model, an icon of class.

Folu Agoi, President of PEN Nigeria, for carving a space for me to share my vision. for your relentless support. many thanks.

Femi Morgan, my comrade. we made it! i'll never forget that day we had a bike accident. you screamed, "Ogungbade! are you okay?" Ha!

Ruby Igwe, you make my heart go *da-dum!*. for being there for me.

Edaoto Agbeniyi, the afrogenius. you are a blessing to Africa.

Bolu Afolabi, our paths may have taken us in different directions, but brothers will forever remain brothers. for always looking out for me, especially when i slip up.

Jahman Anikulapo, for all the good deeds you have done for me.

CPSIA information can be obtained
at www.ICGtesting.com
Printed in the USA
BVHW070711060822
643966BV00008B/1312